Samantha
1904

The Gift

by **Jennifer Hirsch**

Based on stories by Pleasant Rowland, Susan Adler, and Valerie Tripp

★ American Girl®

Samantha's Family and Friends

Grandmary
Samantha's
grandmother, who
is raising her to be
a young lady

Uncle Gard
Samantha's
favorite uncle

Nellie
The girl who
lives—and works—
next door

Hawkins
The butler, who is
Samantha's friend

Mrs. Hawkins
The cook, who
always has a treat
for Samantha

Cornelia
Uncle Gard's friend,
who has modern
ideas about being
a lady

Alice
Cornelia's youngest
sister, who is four
years old

Agnes & Agatha
Cornelia's sisters and
Samantha's newest
friends

Jessie
Grandmary's
seamstress

Elsa
The maid

Table of Contents

Nellie

amantha Parkington leaned over the porch railing and looked out over the broad lawn toward the road, listening for the heavy clip-clop of the milkman's horse, a big dapple-gray named Cloudy. Samantha had saved her apple core for Cloudy. She loved the tickly feeling of the gentle horse taking the apple from her hand. But so far, the road was quiet and empty, except for two young men whizzing by on bicycles. Their bicycles looked so tall and spindly, it was hard to believe they could hold the weight of a rider. *Ridiculous contraptions,* Grandmary called them. Samantha knew her grandmother thought bicycles were dangerous, and she couldn't imagine riding one herself. Even if she could, she was sure Grandmary would say that bicycle riding wasn't ladylike.

Just then, at the big yellow house across the yard, a side door opened and a girl appeared. She was dressed in a gray servant's uniform and carried an enormous wicker basket of laundry. *Why, she doesn't look any older than I am,* thought Samantha, who was nine. *I wonder who she is.*

Samantha heard a clinking noise by the kitchen door.

Mrs. Hawkins, Grandmary's cook, stepped outside carrying a basket of empty milk bottles. She set them down for the milkman to collect.

"What are you doing out here so early this morning, Miss Samantha?" asked Mrs. Hawkins.

"I'm waiting for Cloudy, so I can feed him my apple core," said Samantha. "But look, Mrs. Hawkins—there's a new girl working next door! She seems awfully small to carry such a big basket by herself."

"I'm sure she's accustomed to hard work," Mrs. Hawkins replied. "Not every child is as fortunate as you, Miss Samantha." Mrs. Hawkins went back into the kitchen.

Samantha sighed. Sometimes she couldn't help feeling lonely. She loved her grandmother very much, but it wasn't the same as having a mother and father or brothers and sisters.

Next door, the girl had begun hanging the laundry on long clotheslines. The heavy, wet sheets were much larger than she was, and she had to keep the sheets from touching the ground as she stood on a stool and clipped each sheet corner onto a clothesline with wooden pegs.

Samantha hopped off the porch and crossed the yard to where the girl was working. "May I help?" she asked, picking up a sheet. "It will be easier with two."

"Oh, no, miss—I can do it myself," the girl said quickly. "You mustn't trouble yourself."

"It's no trouble," said Samantha. "I'm just waiting for the milkman, so I might as well help you while I wait. My name is Samantha Parkington," she added, remembering her manners. "Please, what's yours?"

"I'm Nellie O'Malley, miss," the girl said shyly, bobbing in a quick curtsy.

"It's very nice to meet you, Nellie," said Samantha. "When did you begin working here?"

"Two days ago," said Nellie. "I used to live in the city with my family. I was working in a thread factory, but the bad air made me cough, so my parents sent me here to work instead."

"You had to leave your family?" Samantha asked in disbelief. Imagine leaving your family, if you were lucky enough to have one!

"Yes, miss. But things are better for me here," said Nellie. "The air is clean, and I'm not coughing anymore. There's more food to eat here, too, and I can even go to school." She reached for a pillowcase and shook out the wrinkles. "But I do miss my family," she added.

"Well, *I'm* glad you're here," said Samantha. "My parents died when I was five, so I live with Grandmary—that's my grandmother. And I have an uncle who lives in the city." Her eyes lit up. "Say, I've just had the most wonderful idea, Nellie! The next time we go to the city to visit my uncle, you could come with us and visit your family!"

Nellie shook her head. "Oh, thank you, but no, miss. I don't think I'd be permitted to—" Suddenly Nellie went silent, and Samantha felt a hand gripping her shoulder.

"Sakes alive, Miss Samantha, I've been looking all over for you!" It was Elsa, Grandmary's maid, who loved to scold. "Your grandmother wants you. She won't be pleased to know that you've been hobnobbing with servant girls." Elsa jabbed a finger at Nellie. "You there—stick to your work and stop bothering Miss Samantha," she ordered, putting her hand against Samantha's back and steering her toward the house. Samantha quickly tossed her apple core into the bushes and gave Nellie a sorry look.

Elsa led Samantha into the parlor, where Grandmary was sitting in a high-back chair. "Begging your pardon, ma'am, here is Miss Samantha," said Elsa. "I found her next door, hanging laundry with the new servant girl!"

"That will be all, Elsa," said Grandmary. The maid nodded briskly, turned on her heel, and left the parlor.

"Come here, Samantha," said Grandmary. "Would you like to tell me what you were doing next door?"

"Yes, Grandmary," Samantha said earnestly. "I was

helping Nellie with the big sheets. Nellie's quite small, and it was hard for her to hang them all by herself."

"I see," said Grandmary.

"Nellie used to work in a thread factory in the city," Samantha went on, "but the air was making her cough. So her parents sent her here to Mount Bedford to work. I think she's about my same age, and now she lives right next door to us!"

Grandmary looked thoughtful. "I know you mean well, my dear," she said, "but remember, you and Nellie cannot be friends."

Samantha's face fell. "But—but why not?"

"Because you are a proper young lady, and Nellie is

a servant," said Grandmary. "She is not a suitable friend for you."

Samantha hid her disappointment. She knew she must not contradict Grandmary, so she said, "Yes, ma'am. But Nellie is all alone here." She wanted to add, *And so am I,* but instead she said, "It must be hard for her to be so far away from her family."

Grandmary took Samantha's hand in hers. "Perhaps it is. Still, you must respect her position as a servant and not distract her from her responsibilities," Grandmary said gently. Then she squeezed Samantha's hand and said, "Although you may not play with Nellie, you are permitted to *help* her."

Samantha brightened. "That's just what I was doing!"

"Very well, then." Grandmary reached up and straightened Samantha's hair bow. "Now, please go and practice the piano for an hour. Gardner is coming for lunch, and he's bringing his friend Miss Cornelia Pitt." A smile flickered across her face. "If only he wouldn't insist on bringing that noisy automobile, too. How a fine lady such as Miss Pitt can abide being carried about in such a contraption, I simply can't imagine."

Samantha could. Once Uncle Gard had taken her for a ride in his automobile, and she had found it thrilling—so much faster and smoother than riding in a horse-drawn

carriage! Never before had she moved
with such speed! She wondered
what Miss Pitt thought of riding in
an automobile: Did she enjoy it, like
Samantha, or frown on it, like Grandmary?

Samantha went into the music room, settled down at
the piano, and began to play a scale, but her mind wasn't
on the music. She was still thinking about Miss Cornelia
Pitt. Grandmary had told her a little bit about Uncle
Gard's new friend, the lovely young lady named Cornelia.
Samantha was curious about her. But funnily enough, now
that Samantha was going to meet her, she felt uneasy. Her
Uncle Gard was special. He always seemed to understand
Samantha in a way that no one else did, and he always
made her feel as if she was his favorite person in the world.
Would things be the same when Miss Pitt was here, too?
Or would her uncle give this Miss Cornelia Pitt his atten-
tion instead?

With both hands, Samantha banged a C-sharp chord.
C for Cornelia. *I'm not sure I want to meet her after all,*
thought Samantha. Why couldn't Miss Pitt just stay in
New York City and let Samantha have Uncle Gard all to
herself in Mount Bedford?

"Land sakes, Miss Samantha," scolded Elsa, as she
bustled about the music room with her feather duster.

"What has that piano ever done to you that you treat it so severely?"

Samantha flushed as she hurried through the rest of her scales. After Elsa left the room, Samantha closed the lid of the piano and stood up. She went to the window and peeked out, hoping for another glimpse of Nellie. Instead, she heard several noisy pops followed by a loud rumble and the crunch of tires on gravel. A sleek black roadster pulled into the driveway and sputtered to a stop.

"Grandmary!" Samantha called out, too filled with excitement to be proper and ladylike. "It's Uncle Gard! He's here!"

A Gift from Uncle Gard

nstead of waiting for Hawkins, the butler, Samantha pulled open the big front doors herself. She took the steps in a single leap and threw herself into her uncle's arms just as he climbed out of his automobile.

Uncle Gard pretended to stagger under her weight. "My, but you're growing, Sam!" he exclaimed. "I believe you've grown a foot since I saw you last." He set Samantha down and stared at her feet with a concerned frown. "Nope, still only two that I can see. Thank goodness for that. With three feet, you'd have an awfully hard time using the gift we brought you."

"You brought a gift for me?" Samantha asked eagerly. "Thank you!"

Uncle Gard scratched his head. "That is, unless we forgot to bring it. You see, it was all Cornelia's idea." He looked over at Cornelia, who was stepping out of the automobile as Hawkins held open the door for her.

Samantha saw that Cornelia was elegant and pretty, with merry eyes and shining chestnut-brown hair. She wore a long, cream-colored coat and a broad-brimmed hat

with a veil to protect herself from road dust in the open car.

"Did we forget to bring Sam's present?" Uncle Gard asked Cornelia. She shook her head and smiled, and Samantha knew that he was teasing.

Cornelia came up to Samantha. "How lovely to meet you at last," she said. "Gard has told me so much about you."

"How do you do?" Samantha said politely, dipping into a curtsy. "I'm very pleased to meet you, Miss Pitt." Samantha knew it was the right thing to say, but she wasn't sure it was entirely the truth. She glanced at her uncle, who was beaming at his friend. Samantha felt a little twinge of dismay. She could tell that Uncle Gard was very, very fond of Miss Pitt.

"Oh, please call me Cornelia," said Miss Pitt. "You and I need not be so formal."

Grandmary came down the front steps and joined them. "Welcome to Mount Bedford, Cornelia," she said, taking Cornelia's hand in both of hers. Then she tilted her cheek to receive her son's kiss. "Gardner dear, it has been entirely too quiet here without you and your dreadful automobile," she said. Samantha smiled to herself. Even Grandmary joked when Uncle Gard was around!

Uncle Gard smiled broadly. "If my motorcar is too noisy, then you are sure to appreciate the gift we brought for Samantha. It is a perfectly silent form of transportation," he said mysteriously.

Samantha was puzzled. Even a slow, plodding wagon horse like Cloudy made *some* noise.

"Guess what it is, Sam," said Uncle Gard. "It's something you can ride, but it makes no noise."

Samantha thought for moment. "A sled?" she asked.

"Good guess!" Cornelia said to Samantha. "I love sledding. We must go sledding together this winter."

Samantha bit her lip. Sledding had always been something she and Uncle Gard did together.

"A sled *is* a good guess, but it's not the right answer," said Uncle Gard. "Guess again!"

Samantha thought harder. "A rowboat?"

"Nope!" said Uncle Gard. "One more guess."

Suddenly it came to her. "I've got it!" Samantha said. "It's a canoe."

"You're *almost* right," said Uncle Gard. "It's like a canoe—on wheels." With a dramatic whoosh, he pulled the canvas tarp off the back of the automobile. Samantha gasped when she saw what was there: three shiny new bicycles!

Grandmary gasped, too. "My heavens, Gardner. Whatever will Samantha do with *three* bicycles?"

"Have fun, I hope!" said Uncle Gard, winking at Samantha. He lifted a beautiful blue bicycle out of the back of the car and rolled it toward Samantha. "This one is yours, Sam. We're going to keep all three bicycles here in Mount Bedford. Just think of the fun we'll have, you and Cornelia and I, bicycling together."

"I told Gard it was high time you had a bicycle, Samantha," Cornelia chimed in. "I loved cycling when I was your age. It's so fast and free! I'm sure you'll love it, too."

"Oh, thank you," Samantha breathed. She put one hand on the shiny handlebar and the other on the leather seat and looked up at her grandmother. "Please, Grandmary," she asked, "may I keep it?"

Grandmary put her hand on her chest. "In my day, bicycles were ridden in circus acts by women wearing tights," she said, looking a bit scandalized. "Nowadays, of course, women even ride bicycles in the streets. Some wear those dreadful puffy trousers called bloomers. We called them 'bloomer girls.' Can you imagine, women wearing trousers? Most unladylike!"

Cornelia spoke up gently. "I think a lady behaves like a lady no matter what she is wearing. I'm sure Samantha will never behave improperly on her bicycle."

"Indeed not!" Grandmary replied tartly. She turned to

Samantha. "My dear, I can see that you have your heart set on riding this bicycle with Gardner and Cornelia," she said. "You may keep it if you promise to be careful."

"I will," Samantha promised.

❧

After lunch, Uncle Gard said, "Well, Sam, shall we take your new bicycle out for a spin?"

"Oh, yes, please," Samantha said eagerly, leading Uncle Gard and Cornelia out to the driveway, where the three bicycles stood waiting.

"Well, hop on, Sam," said Uncle Gard. He held the blue bicycle as Samantha climbed on and settled onto the seat. The skirts of her dress and her pinafore and her petticoats billowed around her. She tucked them all under her legs to get them out of the way. Then Uncle Gard pushed, and she pedaled, and the wheels turned—and there she was, riding the bicycle, with Uncle Gard running alongside to hold her steady.

"Hurray!" Cornelia cheered.

The ruffles on Samantha's pinafore fluttered, and her heart did, too. Riding a bicycle was harder than she had thought it would be. She tried to keep the front tire from wobbling, and she tried to keep a smile on her face, but she was afraid she would topple over if not for Uncle Gard's firm hold.

There she was, riding the bicycle, with Uncle Gard
running alongside, holding her steady.

After a few minutes, Uncle Gard asked, "Are you ready for me to let go?"

Samantha gulped, but she wanted to impress her uncle and Cornelia, so she nodded. Uncle Gard let go, and she rode the bike in a wide, wobbly circle on the driveway.

When she stopped, Uncle Gard and Cornelia clapped and cheered. Grandmary came out and joined them.

"I knew you'd get the hang of it right away!" Cornelia praised her.

"Let's go to the park," Uncle Gard suggested with enthusiasm. "There are lots of paths there, so you won't have to go round in circles."

"Dear me!" said Grandmary. "Don't you think it's a bit too soon?"

"I think it's up to Sam," said Uncle Gard. "If she's plucky enough to try the park, then we should let her. What do you say, Sam?"

Samantha was not sure she wanted to go to the park, but she *was* sure she wanted to be plucky. "Let's go," she said.

"That's my girl!" said Uncle Gard proudly.

The park was crowded with bicyclists enjoying the sunny fall day. Samantha thought they were all cycling rather fast, as if their bicycles were being hurried along by the brisk breeze.

"You go first, Sam," said Uncle Gard as they wheeled their bicycles to the path that ran alongside the lake. "Cornelia and I will follow and keep an eye on you."

"All right," said Samantha. Feeling awkward and unsteady, she mounted her bicycle. She wanted to tuck her skirts out of the way, but there wasn't time. Her bicycle began rolling forward before she had even started pedaling!

The path wasn't as flat as Grandmary's driveway. To Samantha's right, the path sloped toward the shore of the lake. Samantha pedaled slowly, concentrating as hard as she could on not falling. Suddenly she felt a tug. She looked down. Her skirt had caught in the bicycle chain! She started to yank it free just as Uncle Gard shouted, "Watch out!"

Samantha looked up. A young man on a bicycle was flying straight toward her at top speed. In a panic, Samantha swerved hard to the right. Her bike lurched off the path and bounced down the bank, out of control.

"Help!" she shrieked. She struggled to steer, but the front wheel wobbled as the bicycle went faster and faster. *Splash!* Samantha and the bicycle fell right into the mucky water at the edge of the lake.

"Samantha!" shouted Uncle Gard and Cornelia as they rushed down the slope to help her. "Are you all right?"

Samantha nodded, although she was fighting back tears. Her ankle was scraped and her stockings were torn. Her pinafore was mud-spattered, grass-stained, and grease-streaked, and her petticoat was so badly twisted around the chain that she had to rip it to get it free. Whatever would she say to Grandmary? If Grandmary knew that she had fallen and hurt herself, she might decide bicycles were too dangerous for Samantha. And that wasn't even the worst of it.

No, the worst thing was that Samantha felt utterly humiliated. She thought of what Cornelia had said: *I loved cycling when I was your age. It's so fast and free!* Samantha looked down at herself. She was not fast and free—she was a tangled, torn, and muddy mess. A tear ran down her cheek before she could stop it.

"Buck up, Sam," said Uncle Gard, as they walked their bicycles back to the house. "We'll go for a ride together next time Cornelia and I come to Mount Bedford. Meanwhile, you'll have time to practice."

Practice? Next time? thought Samantha. *I never want to get on that bicycle again as long as I live!*

꧂

That evening, after Uncle Gard and Cornelia had left and Samantha had finished a quiet supper with Grandmary, she went out to the back porch. Tomorrow would be Sunday—which meant that servants would have the afternoon off. So Samantha sat down on the steps and watched the yellow house next door like a hawk, hoping she would see Nellie.

The daylight was fading, and Samantha was nearly ready to give up when she heard a door close and Nellie came outside carrying a metal bucket. She went to the ash can at the side of the house and emptied her bucket into it. Samantha got up and hurried across the yard.

"Nellie, wait!" she called softly.

Nellie looked up, surprised. "What is it, miss?"

Samantha caught up to her by the ash can. "Nellie, do you have the afternoon off tomorrow?" she asked.

"Yes, miss. I'm off at one o'clock on Sundays," Nellie replied.

"Then let's meet," said Samantha. "I know a secret place where no one will see us!"

Nellie hesitated. "Where?" she asked.

Samantha pointed to the shrubbery that divided the lawn between the two houses. "See that big lilac hedge? Near the chestnut tree, there's a hole in the hedge that connects our yards, and you can crawl right in. It's like a hidden tunnel. Nobody will see us there!" she whispered. "That's where I'll be waiting for you."

Nellie nodded, her eyes sparkling. "I'll see you tomorrow, miss!"

Lydia

unday morning seemed to crawl by. After
church, Samantha practiced her piano diligently
and then worked on her sampler of stitches until lunch-
time. Finally, lunch was over. Samantha slipped two of the
ginger cookies that Mrs. Hawkins had served for dessert
into her pinafore pocket before anyone noticed. Then she
laid her silverware across the side of her plate and folded
her linen napkin to show that she was finished.

"May I please be excused?" she asked politely, and
Grandmary nodded.

Samantha ran upstairs to her bedroom. She selected her
very best doll and wrapped her in a doll blanket. Carrying
her bundle, she went quietly out the front door. She knew
that if she went through the kitchen to the back door, Mrs.
Hawkins might see her. Once she was on the veranda,
Samantha tiptoed around the side of the house and down
the back steps, glancing over her shoulder to be sure
nobody was watching. Then she raced across the lawn to
the lilac hedge and crawled into the opening.

"Nellie, are you here? It's me, Samantha," she called

softly. No one answered. Careful to hold her doll away from the spiky branches, Samantha crawled through the tunnel. Suddenly she heard a rustle up ahead, and there was Nellie, her eyes glinting with excitement.

"Here's my secret hiding place!" said Samantha. On her hands and knees, she led Nellie into a slightly wider opening deep inside the hedge. The sunlight coming through the branches made the leaves glow green. Samantha sat down, took the ginger cookies from her pocket, and handed one to Nellie.

After they had eaten the cookies, Samantha carefully unwrapped her bundle.

At the sight of the beautiful doll, Nellie's eyes grew wide. She caught her breath and whispered, "Oh!"

"Would you like to hold her?" Samantha asked.

Nellie couldn't speak. She simply gazed at the doll.

"This doll was a gift from my grandmother," Samantha said as she set the doll in Nellie's lap. "Her name is Lydia. That was my mother's name."

Nellie carefully reached down and touched Lydia's lacy bonnet and the tiny buttons on her frock. "Oh, she's so pretty and sweet! She reminds me of my dear little sisters," Nellie said softly. "How I miss them." Her eyes shining, Nellie bent down and kissed Lydia on her plump, rosy cheek.

"I always wanted to have a sister," Samantha said wistfully. "You're lucky. How many sisters do you have?"

"Two," said Nellie. "Bridget is six, and Jenny is four."

"You must miss them very much," said Samantha.

Nellie nodded. Samantha thought she saw Nellie's lip tremble. Nellie picked up Lydia and hugged her tightly.

Samantha felt sorry that she had brought up such a tender subject. She tried to think of a topic that wouldn't remind Nellie of her family and how much she missed them. "Will you go to school tomorrow?" she asked.

Nellie nodded again.

"Will you attend Miss Crampton's Academy? That's where I go," Samantha said hopefully.

"I don't think so," said Nellie. "I think it's called Mount Bedford Public School."

"Oh, I know where that school is. It's not far from Miss Crampton's," said Samantha. "I pass it on my way. In the afternoon as I'm walking home, I always hear the bell ring and see the students leaving. I could meet you on the corner, and we could walk home together."

Nellie looked up. Her eyelashes were damp, but she was smiling. "I'd like that," she said.

"So would I," said Samantha.

🐚

Monday afternoon, Samantha left Miss Crampton's Academy and walked to Mount Bedford Public School. Just as she was crossing the street to the school, she heard the end-of-day bell ring, and students began streaming out of the doors, laughing and calling to one another. Samantha hurried to the far corner at the end of the block, where she and Nellie had arranged to meet. When she arrived, Nellie was kneeling in the grass, her face in her hands and her shoulders shaking.

Samantha stopped beside her. "Nellie?" she asked. "What's wrong?"

Nellie didn't reply.

Samantha knelt down and put her arm around Nellie's shoulders. "Please, will you tell me what happened?"

"I can't read very well," Nellie sobbed. "All the other students in my class are younger than I am—and smarter, too. They laugh at me and call me dummy when I make mistakes."

Samantha frowned. "Doesn't the teacher do anything?"

"The teacher says I should be in first grade, not second," said Nellie. "She says I'm too far behind." She added, "Maybe I don't belong in school after all. I'll never catch up."

"Nonsense—of course you will," Samantha said stoutly. "Now, let's go home and—"

Just then, a girl's voice said, "Hello, Samantha." Samantha turned to see two of her classmates, Edith Eddleton and Helen Whitney, walking home with their arms linked. "Who is your friend?" asked Edith.

"This is Nellie O'Malley," Samantha told them. "Nellie, this is—" but before she could introduce her schoolmates, Helen spoke up.

"Why, she's dressed like a servant!" Helen exclaimed.

"So she is," said Edith, wrinkling her nose. "Come along, Helen. *We* don't consort with servant girls." Edith tugged Helen's arm, and they turned and walked away.

"Don't pay them any mind, Nellie," said Samantha. "And don't let the students in your class bother you either. I'm sure you'll do better tomorrow. New things are always hard at first. Now, buck up, as my uncle would say." Nellie stood up and wiped her tears, and Samantha helped her gather up her books and lunch bucket.

"Tell me about your uncle," said Nellie, as the girls set off. "Is he the one who lives in the city? What is he like?"

"Yes," said Samantha. "He's my mother's brother, and he's my favorite person in the world. He's clever and funny and smart and kind."

"He sounds wonderful," said Nellie.

"He is," said Samantha. "I wish you could meet him. I just know you'd like him, and I bet he'd like you, too."

The girls had reached the house where Nellie was staying and working. Samantha told her, "Now, as soon as your afternoon chores are finished, come and meet me at the kitchen door. I'll be waiting for you on the porch, right there," she said, pointing across the lawn to the back porch of her house. "I have an idea."

"What sort of idea?" Nellie asked.

"You'll see!" Samantha replied mysteriously.

❧

Samantha went up to her room and changed out of her school clothes. Then she went downstairs to the parlor to find her grandmother.

"Good afternoon, Grandmary," she said with a small curtsy.

"Good afternoon, my dear," said Grandmary, smiling. "Please sit down and tell me about your day."

"Well," said Samantha. "I have decided that I want to start my own school."

"Goodness gracious, Samantha," said Grandmary. "Do you mean to say you have already learned everything that Miss Crampton has to teach you?"

"Oh, it's not a school for me. It's for Nellie," Samantha explained. "She needs help with reading and doing arithmetic so that she can move up to the third grade, where she belongs."

"I see," said Grandmary.

"Would it be all right if Nellie were to come here when she finishes her work?" Samantha asked.

Grandmary hesitated. Then she said, "Since you will be *helping* Nellie, it is acceptable for her to come over here to take lessons from you."

"Thank you, Grandmary," said Samantha gratefully. "I will do my very best to be a good teacher to Nellie."

"I am sure Nellie will learn a great deal from you," said Grandmary.

꧁

Later that afternoon, Samantha met Nellie at the kitchen door. She led Nellie up two flights of stairs and into a little room in the tower at the very top of the house.

It was sunny and private, with windows on all four sides that looked out over the treetops. On a cozy window seat, Samantha had set some picture books, a slate for writing, a jar of beans for counting, and her doll, Lydia. Nellie immediately sat down on the seat beside the doll.

"Lydia needs to practice her sums," Samantha joked. "I keep asking her what two and two is, but she never answers. I guess she doesn't know!"

Nellie smiled. "Even I know the answer to that."

In fact, Samantha discovered that Nellie was very good at arithmetic. She could add and subtract numbers in her head faster than Samantha could count out the beans or even write the numbers on the slate.

"Jiminy, you're quick with sums!" she told Nellie. "You're already doing third-grade work in math."

"In the city, I often did the shopping when my mother was busy at home," said Nellie. "I had to know how much I could buy with the money I had—and make sure the shopkeeper gave me the right amount of change."

"Well, then, all we need to do is work on your reading, and you'll move up to third grade in no time," said Samantha. She opened her favorite book, *The Wonderful Wizard of Oz*, and read the first sentence aloud: "'Dorothy lived in the midst of the great Kansas prairies, with Uncle Henry, who was a farmer, and Aunt Em, who was the farmer's wife.'" Samantha passed the book to Nellie. "Here, Nellie, now you read a line," she said.

The girls read an entire chapter that way, passing the book back and forth. At first, Nellie needed help with many of the words. As the sun sank lower in the sky, they came to the part about the cyclone, and Nellie didn't want to stop. The light in the attic room turned golden as Nellie read the last line of the chapter with only a little help on the longer words: "'In spite of the swaying of the house

Samantha passed the book to Nellie. "Here, Nellie,
now you read a line," she said.

and the wailing of the wind, Dorothy soon closed her eyes and fell fast asleep.'"

With a sigh of happiness, Nellie closed the book and handed it back to Samantha. "Oh, what will happen to Dorothy and Toto?"

"Strange and wonderful things," Samantha promised. "Now, you'd best hurry home before anyone misses you next door, so that you can come again tomorrow."

As the girls went down the back stairs, Nellie said, "You're a good teacher, Samantha. I like your class better than my class at Mount Bedford School."

"We'll call ours Mount *Better* School!" Samantha said with a grin.

The Speaking Contest

he next day at Miss Crampton's Academy, Samantha noticed Edith glancing at her and then whispering to Helen and the other girls. Curious and a bit suspicious, Samantha marched right up to Edith. "What's all this about?" she asked boldly.

"Why, hello, Samantha," said Edith. "How is your friend the servant girl?" Edith glanced around at the other girls and then asked, "Is she teaching you how to peel potatoes?" The other girls tittered.

Samantha's eyes narrowed. "I'd rather peel potatoes with Nellie than pick posies with you nincompoops," she retorted.

Edith flushed. "I wonder what others would have to say if they knew about your servant friend," she sputtered.

"Go ahead and tell anyone you like," Samantha replied.

At the front of the room, Miss Crampton tapped a gavel on her desk. "Young ladies, it is time to take your seats," she said. "I'm pleased to announce that soon you will all be participating in a speaking contest! The Mount Bedford Ladies Club sponsors this event every year. This year, the topic they have chosen is 'Progress in America.' That is what your speeches will be about."

The class murmured with excitement.

"And that's not all," Miss Crampton went on. "The two students with the best speeches will present their speeches at a public assembly at the Mount Bedford Opera House, along with the winning students from the boys' academy and the public school. The mayor and other important members of our community will be in the audience to hear the winning speeches." All the girls clapped. "Now," said Miss Crampton, "open your notebooks, and let's get started."

Samantha picked up her pencil and thought about the topic, "Progress in America." What was progress, anyway? After all, she thought, the very things that some people viewed as progress, such as Hawkins's telephone or Elsa's

Telephone

vacuum cleaner or Uncle Gard's automobile, were the very same things that others, like Grandmary, viewed as noisy and uncivilized. *Newfangled contraptions*, she called them. Samantha felt quite sure that Grandmary did not consider such things to be signs of progress in America.

Thinking about Uncle Gard's automobile made Samantha think about New York

City, where he lived. He had told Samantha about the city's great factories that sent goods all around the world, and how people from all over the world came to live in New York City, just so they could work in those very factories. Surely anyone, even Grandmary, would agree that factories were a true sign of progress in America!

Samantha opened her notebook to a clean page and began to write.

⁊❧

At school the following day, Miss Crampton announced, "Young ladies, now that you have finished writing your speeches, you will each present your speech to the class. Stand up, look at your audience, and speak clearly."

One by one, the girls took turns giving their speeches to the class. Helen talked about electrical lights and how much safer and cleaner they were than gas-lights. Edith thrilled the class with a report on the  Wright Brothers of Kitty Hawk, North Carolina, who had invented a flying machine!

After each student spoke, Miss Crampton praised the speech and gave tips on what she called *elocution*. "Remember to enunciate each word, use expression, and speak more loudly and slowly than usual."

When Samantha's name was called, she stood up and read aloud the speech she had written: "In America, our big cities like New York are famous for their factories. People come here from all over the world so that they can work in American factories. Our factories make important things that people need, like clothing and canned food. They make useful things that everyone needs, like paper and soap. They make wonderful new inventions like the telephone, so that we can talk over long distances, and inventions that let people travel faster, like the automobile and bicycle. Although a lot of people still prefer horses," she added, and the students smiled and nodded. Samantha knew the girls in her class liked horses as much as she did. "In America, our factories are proof of our progress."

All the students applauded with enthusiasm, and Samantha flushed with pride. She especially liked the punchy way her speech ended, with "proof of our progress." Maybe factories weren't as interesting or exciting as flying machines, but she could tell that the class had liked her speech.

"Thank you, Samantha. Anyone who hears that speech would surely agree with you that factories are a sign of progress in America," Miss Crampton praised her.

After the last speech, Miss Crampton announced

the two winners. "Congratulations on your excellent speeches, Edith Eddleton and Samantha Parkington," said the teacher. She looked around at the class. "Edith and Samantha will present their speeches to the public at the opera house this Saturday, at one o'clock. You and your families are all invited."

☙

Walking home that afternoon, Samantha felt as if she were floating on air. As soon as she got home, she told Grandmary about her speech and the public assembly on Saturday.

"Well done, Samantha," said Grandmary. "I very much look forward to hearing your speech! And now, run along and practice your piano. Practice makes perfect."

"Yes, Grandmary," said Samantha, eager to be finished with piano practice before Nellie arrived for her lessons.

At the piano, Samantha's fingers flew through the scales without a single mistake, and even her most challenging piece suddenly seemed easier to play. *Practice makes perfect* was one of Grandmary's favorite sayings. Samantha had always regarded it as something grown-ups said to make you do things you didn't want to do—like practicing penmanship or stitching a sampler—but she realized that the saying might actually be true. Maybe, she thought, practice would make her bicycle riding perfect, too.

The front doorbell rang. Samantha lifted her hands from the keyboard, curious to know who the caller was. Nellie wouldn't be here so soon, and she wouldn't use the front door, so it couldn't be her. Through the door of the music room, Samantha saw Hawkins usher three well-dressed ladies into the parlor. A few minutes later, Elsa crossed the hall from the kitchen carrying a tea tray. She, too, disappeared into the parlor.

Samantha got up from the piano and went to the door of the music room. In the parlor, the ladies were discussing dull topics like the weather and the delicious oatmeal cookies Mrs. Hawkins had baked. *I must get a few of those for Nellie and me*, Samantha thought to herself, when she heard her name mentioned. She tiptoed across the hall and peeked into the parlor.

"I beg your pardon, Mrs. Edwards, but I'm afraid I have bad news," said one of the ladies in a disapproving tone. "It seems that your granddaughter has been keeping company with a servant girl."

"You don't say," Grandmary replied mildly. "Where did you hear this report?"

"My daughter Edith saw Samantha after school in the company of a servant girl," said the lady. "Edith is most concerned."

"What a state of affairs!" "Where will it all lead?" the

"I beg your pardon, Mrs. Edwards, but I'm afraid I have bad news,"
said one of the ladies in a disapproving tone.

other ladies murmured, shaking their heads.

That Edith! thought Samantha. *What business is it of hers?*

Grandmary's back was rigid, but her voice was soft.
"Samantha is tutoring young Nellie, who does not have
the same advantage our children do, of attending Miss
Crampton's fine academy." Grandmary took a sip of tea
and looked around at the other ladies. "Surely, we can
all admire this generosity of spirit toward the poor and
disadvantaged?"

Nobody spoke. Finally the other ladies nodded in
agreement.

"I'm so glad we cleared that up," Grandmary said
calmly. "More tea, anyone?"

"Miss Samantha!" It was Mrs. Hawkins calling her
from the kitchen. Quickly, before she was seen at the parlor
door, Samantha hurried down the hall and through the
kitchen to find Nellie standing at the back door. As Mrs.
Hawkins let Nellie in, Samantha helped herself to a few
of the oatmeal cookies that were cooling on the counter
and stuffed them into the pocket of her pinafore. Then the
girls trotted two flights up the back staircase and arrived,
breathless and giddy, in the tower room.

"Welcome back to Mount Better School!" said
Samantha, handing Nellie a cookie.

Nellie settled happily into the window seat and

offered a bite of her cookie to Lydia.

"Why thank you, Miss Nellie," said Samantha in a high voice, pretending to be Lydia. "These are very delicious cookies. And isn't the weather fine and sunny today?"

"Oh, indeed it is, Lydia," Nellie answered, as the girls giggled with amusement.

When they had finished their cookies, Nellie opened *The Wonderful Wizard of Oz* and began to read aloud. Again, at first she stumbled over the longer words, but with Samantha's help, her reading became smoother and smoother. By the end of chapter two, she needed very little help.

"Well done, Nellie," said Samantha. "You see? Practice makes perfect. That's what Grandmary always says, and she's usually right about things." Then Samantha told Nellie about the speaking contest and the public assembly. "So I should practice my speech! May I read it to you?"

Nellie nodded. "Oh, yes, please! I'd love to hear it. Lydia and I will listen together," said Nellie, lifting the doll onto her lap and looking expectantly at Samantha.

Samantha stood up, opened her school notebook, and read her speech out loud just as she had in school. "In America, our factories are proof of our progress," she finished, closing her notebook and looking up at her audience of one.

But Nellie wasn't smiling. She didn't clap. She was looking down at Lydia, smoothing the doll's hair over and over.

"Nellie? Didn't you like my speech?" Samantha asked.

Nellie shrugged. "It's fine, I suppose." She still did not
look at Samantha.

Samantha could see that something was wrong. "What
did you *really* think of my speech, Nellie?" she asked.
"Please tell me."

Nellie looked up at her. "It's full of nice words," she
said quietly. "They just don't tell the real truth."

"They don't? What do you mean?" asked Samantha,
curious.

"I used to work in a thread factory with a lot of other
children," said Nellie. "We worked twelve hours a day,
six days a week. The bosses liked to hire children because
they could pay us less, and our fingers are small so we
could tie knots in the thread whenever it broke on the big
spools. Children are light, so we could climb up onto the
machines if something needed to be fixed. But climbing
the machines is easier without shoes, so we had to work
barefoot, and the factory floors were very, very cold in the
winter. My feet would get numb. And the dust from all
the bits of thread floating in the air made me cough all the
time, even when I was at home." Still stroking Lydia's hair,
Nellie continued, "The big thread machines were loud and

dangerous. Once, I saw a girl's hair get caught in a thread spool. It ripped half her scalp off."

Samantha caught her breath. "How awful," she whispered. Her chest ached, as if the thought of all those poor children working in factories had made her heart hurt. Thankfully, Nellie was no longer one of them. But Uncle Gard had told her that big cities like New York had many factories—so surely there must be hundreds, even thousands, of children working in them.

"That's why I'm glad to be working as a housemaid here in Mount Bedford, even if it means I'm far away from my family," said Nellie.

"Oh, Nellie, I—I never knew such terrible things," Samantha exclaimed. Did Uncle Gard know of such things? she wondered. Did Grandmary? One thing was certain—they didn't teach anything about this at Miss Crampton's Academy.

A New Thought

t dinner that evening, Samantha was quiet and not very hungry. She couldn't stop thinking about Nellie's description of working in the thread factory. When Samantha was overly talkative at meals, Grandmary would remind her that "children should be seen and not heard," but tonight, no reminder was needed.

Finally, as the main course was being cleared away along with Samantha's half-eaten plate of food, Grandmary leaned toward her and said, "My dear, are you feeling quite well?"

"Yes, Grandmary," Samantha replied.

"Perhaps you're tired," said Grandmary. "I hope that tutoring Nellie is not too much effort for you."

"No, not at all," said Samantha, sitting up straight and trying to look perky. "I'm learning—I mean, I'm *teaching* Nellie lots of things. She's a quick learner. Her reading has already improved."

"That's good to hear," said Grandmary. "I have some good news to share, too: I received a telephone call from Gardner today. He informed me that he and Cornelia will visit us again on the weekend."

"Oh, that will be very nice," said Samantha, with more politeness than enthusiasm. She was still not sure she liked sharing Uncle Gard with Cornelia.

"I knew you'd be pleased," said Grandmary. "Gardner wanted me to tell you that they're looking forward to cycling with you." She added, "I'm not convinced those circus contraptions are safe for children, but Gardner insists."

Samantha's heart sank. She had not so much as looked at her bicycle since falling off of it into the lake. Carefully, she folded her napkin. "Grandmary, may I please be excused?" she asked.

"Yes, you may," said Grandmary with a nod. As Samantha passed by her chair, Grandmary put a hand on her arm. "My dear, if you would like to practice riding your bicycle, Hawkins can help you. You may ask him for assistance."

"No," said Samantha. "I mean, no thank you. I . . . I have schoolwork to do."

"Very well," said Grandmary. "Best get to it then."

Samantha trudged upstairs to her room, deep in misery. She wanted to tell Grandmary that she was afraid to ride the bicycle again, but the truth was, she felt ashamed. Whenever she thought of her fall in the park, she shivered.

If only she had broken some bones—or broken the bicycle! Then nobody would expect her to ride it.

Samantha pictured herself standing with Grandmary on the veranda, waving good-bye to Uncle Gard and Cornelia as they rode off merrily on bicycles, leaving her behind. That was an awful thought. Samantha wasn't sure which was worse—her fear of getting back on the bicycle or the idea of being left out of the fun with Uncle Gard and Cornelia. If only they had never brought the bicycles to Mount Bedford! How could Samantha tell them that the three of them would never ride together again because she was afraid?

Samantha slumped at her desk, feeling like a failure. She knew that slumping wasn't ladylike, but she was too downhearted to care. She had a page of sums to do before tomorrow, but instead, to cheer herself up, she decided to reread her speech. At least *that* was not a failure! But as she read, Nellie's words about working in the factory kept echoing in her brain. And then, suddenly, a new thought popped into her head: *If Grandmary thinks bicycles are not safe for children, what about factories? Does she think factories are safe for children?*

Samantha sat up straight. She turned to a new page in her notebook and picked up her pen.

⚬

On Wednesday afternoon, Nellie had to polish silver until it was time to set the table for dinner at her house, so there would be no Mount Better School that day. Instead, when Samantha got home from school, she went straight to the carriage house. She found her blue bicycle and wheeled it out to the driveway, determined not to let it get the better of her.

Pushing her skirt and petticoat out of the way, Samantha took a deep breath and swung herself onto the seat. She pushed down on one pedal, and the bicycle rolled forward. Then she pushed the other pedal. So far, so good! Slowly, Samantha kept pedaling, fighting to keep her balance. Suddenly she felt a tug on her skirt. The front tire wobbled, and she tipped over onto the driveway.

Samantha stood up and brushed dirt and gravel off her hands. She wasn't hurt, but she saw that her pinafore was still caught in the bicycle chain. She tugged at it until it came free with the unmistakable sound of ripping fabric.

"Oh!" Samantha groaned in exasperation. Now Grandmary would be displeased. *Well, better to tear my pinafore than break my neck*, she thought bitterly.

Samantha glanced around. Nobody had seen her. *Since I've already torn my pinafore, the damage is done, so I may as well keep trying*, she decided. Bravely she climbed back onto the seat. This time she felt less wobbly and better balanced as she pedaled. But once again, as soon as the bicycle began to pick up speed, her skirt caught the chain, the bicycle tipped over, and *crash!* She tumbled to the ground.

Samantha yanked her skirt loose and climbed on again, her anger giving her gumption. Again, the same thing happened—and this time, when she pulled her pinafore loose, the chain came with it, sliding off the sprockets. It dangled uselessly at the side of the bicycle. Samantha gulped. Now she couldn't ride her bicycle at all!

Samantha wheeled the bicycle back to the carriage house, tears of shame and frustration sliding down her cheeks.

In the carriage house, Hawkins hurried to her side. "Miss Samantha, are you hurt?" he asked, taking the bicycle from her.

"No, but I tore my pinafore and broke the bicycle," said Samantha. "I just can't ride this stupid bicycle. Every time I try, my clothing gets tangled in the chain, and I fall off." She sighed. "Uncle Gard thinks I'm plucky, but I'm not. The truth is, I'm afraid."

"And yet you tried again and again just now, despite your fear," said Hawkins.

"Uncle Gard and Cornelia want to ride bicycles together when they come to visit this weekend," Samantha explained. "If I can't ride with them ..."

"You'll be left out of the fun," Hawkins finished the thought.

Samantha nodded miserably. "And now look what I've done. The chain has come off, and the bicycle can't be ridden at all," she said, trying not to cry. "Uncle Gard will think I am a coward *and* that I was very careless with his gift."

"The chain is easily fixed," said Hawkins. "You just leave this bicycle with me, Miss Samantha, and I'll have it right as rain in no time. Now dry your tears and go ask Jessie to mend your clothing and wash out the grease stains before a certain someone sees it." Samantha knew he meant Grandmary. Hawkins gave her a wink and a pat, and she managed a watery smile in return.

Samantha slipped into the house and up the back stairs before Grandmary saw her. She knocked on the door of the sewing room.

"Come in," Jessie called. Jessie was Grandmary's seamstress, and she was used to patching Samantha up after a mishap. She looked up from her sewing machine as Samantha stepped into the room. "Why, Miss Samantha, don't you look a sight!" she exclaimed.

Samantha held up her torn pinafore, and Jessie examined it. Jessie regarded Samantha from head to toe, turning

her around to look at her from all sides. "Well, nothing
here that a little soap and water and thread can't fix. Leave
your torn clothes with me," she said, helping Samantha
out of her dress and pinafore. "Ring for Elsa and ask her to
draw you a bath. Let's get you cleaned up and presentable
by dinnertime."

"Thank you, Jessie," said Samantha, grateful for her
kindness. Then she hurried down the hall to her bedroom
in her petticoat and rang for Elsa.

By dinnertime, Samantha had cheered up a bit. A hot
bath was always comforting, and the first course at dinner
that evening was Mrs. Hawkins's oyster soup, which was

one of Samantha's favorites. And, bicycle or no bicycle, she couldn't help looking forward to Uncle Gard's visit in a few days. Even if Cornelia would be there, too.

Grandmary also seemed to be thinking about his visit. She remarked, "Gardner is certainly bringing Miss Pitt to visit us again very soon. I wonder what the reason could be."

"Perhaps he misses us," said Samantha.

"No doubt," said Grandmary, "although he hasn't visited with such frequency in the past."

"Maybe it's because of Cornelia," said Samantha.

"That's just what I was thinking," Grandmary said with a smile.

"Cornelia loves cycling, so I expect they're eager to ride their bicycles," Samantha reasoned. Suddenly, her dread at the prospect of another humiliating and painful fall on her bicycle was replaced with a happy realization: On Saturday, she would be so busy practicing and then giving her speech that there would be no time for her to go cycling. Samantha felt more glad than ever to be one of the winners of the speaking contest, even if it did mean sharing the stage with that annoying tattletale Edith Eddleton.

"I'm not sure the bicycles entirely explain it," Grandmary said thoughtfully, setting down her soup spoon and delicately dabbing her lips with her linen napkin.

"Pardon? The bicycles don't explain what?" asked Samantha, confused.

"Well, what I mean to say is—" Grandmary paused, as if she wasn't quite sure how to put it. "Gardner seems to be getting quite serious about Miss Pitt," she said at last.

"Serious?" said Samantha. "But Uncle Gard is always teasing and laughing and telling jokes. He isn't one bit serious, not ever!"

Grandmary smiled and didn't argue. All she said was, "We shall see."

A Matched Pair

aturday morning dawned bright and beautiful.
Shortly after breakfast, Samantha was in the
music room practicing her scales when she heard the
rumble of a motorcar coming up the driveway. She jumped
up and rushed to the window.

"It's Uncle Gard!" she called to Grandmary, as Hawkins
opened the front door. Samantha bounded out onto the
veranda.

Uncle Gard and Cornelia were coming up the front
steps. "Hello, Sam!" said her uncle, greeting her with a
hug. "It's just the day for a bike ride, don't you think?"

Samantha glanced down at her torn and mended
pinafore. "Uncle Gard, I, um, I . . ." she faltered. Then she
remembered her excuse: "Guess what—my speech was one
of the winners in the speaking contest at school!"

"Why, Sam, that's wonderful!" said Uncle Gard.

"Congratulations!" said Cornelia.

"I'm delivering the speech at a public assembly this
afternoon," Samantha continued. "It's at the Mount
Bedford Opera House."

Uncle Gard and Cornelia were coming up the front steps.

"This very afternoon? What excellent timing," said Uncle Gard. "That means Cornelia and I can be in the audience!"

"We certainly wouldn't want to miss it," Cornelia agreed.

"So this morning I'll be very busy practicing my speech for the assembly," Samantha said. "Which means I can't go bicycle riding with you, I'm afraid."

"Are you sure?" Uncle Gard asked. "Hawkins tells me that you've been practicing and doing quite well. When we spoke on the telephone a few days ago, he gave me a full report on your progress."

Samantha looked over at Hawkins. He was lifting a carpetbag out of the car and didn't seem to be paying any attention to their conversation.

"I've been looking forward to cycling with you," said Cornelia.

Uncle Gard grinned. "Cornelia even brought along her special cycling outfit," he said. "Just wait till you see it!"

"And I brought a matching outfit just for you, Samantha," Cornelia said. "It seems a pity you won't be able to wear it today."

Samantha couldn't help feeling curious. "A special cycling outfit?" she asked.

"That's right!" Cornelia said gaily. "Shall we go and see

if it fits you?" She offered her hand, and Samantha took it. Together they went upstairs, bubbling with high spirits. Hawkins followed with a dignified expression, carrying the carpetbag.

In Samantha's bedroom, Cornelia opened the bag. She held up a piece of clothing, and the item unfolded to reveal a pair of baggy pantaloons. Samantha giggled, and Cornelia caught her eye and grinned. "Those are for me—and these are for you," she said, withdrawing a smaller pair of pantaloons, unfolding them, and handing them to Samantha. "Shall we try them on?"

"Yes, please," said Samantha.

Cornelia helped Samantha remove her petticoats and frock, and then she stepped out of her own skirt. Samantha couldn't stop giggling as she and Cornelia pulled on the strange pantaloons. They were gray and puffed out around their legs like big poufy knickers, the kind that boys wore. Samantha looked at herself and Cornelia in the mirror. "We look like two circus clowns!" she exclaimed, laughing.

Cornelia smiled. "These are called bloomers," she said. "They may look silly, but they won't get caught in a bicycle chain."

"Oh!" Samantha gasped. "Why, these must be the 'dreadful puffy trousers' that Grandmary talked about the last time you were here!"

"That's right," said Cornelia. "But your grandmother wants you to be safe, and these are much safer than a skirt for riding a bicycle."

Cornelia and Samantha went back downstairs and out to the veranda, where Uncle Gard and Grandmary were chatting. They looked up as Samantha and Cornelia joined them. Grandmary said nothing, but Uncle Gard said heartily, "Well, well, well! Look at this! My two favorite young ladies, and they're a perfect matched pair!"

Cornelia turned to Grandmary. "I brought a borrowed pair of bloomers for Samantha," she said. "My younger sisters find that bloomers make riding a bicycle easier and safer. I'm hoping Samantha might give them a try."

If Grandmary was surprised, she didn't show it. "How very thoughtful," she murmured. "Perhaps they will mean less wear and tear on Samantha's clothing, and less repair work for Jessie."

Now it was Samantha's turn to be surprised. Did Grandmary somehow know about her torn skirts and pinafore? And—was it really possible that Grandmary would allow her to be a *bloomer girl*?

"May I try them, Grandmary?" Samantha asked.

"You may," said Grandmary. "After all, a lady behaves like a lady no matter what she's wearing," she added, her eyes twinkling at Cornelia. "But the bicycle is still unsteady, so you must still use care," she cautioned.

Hawkins wheeled the blue bicycle up to the front steps. The chain whirred on the sprockets, as good as new. "Climb aboard, Miss Samantha, and let's see how you do now," Hawkins instructed her, holding the bicycle steady.

Samantha took a deep breath. *Be plucky!* she told herself as she settled onto the seat. She pushed one pedal and then the other as the bicycle rolled forward, wobbling only the littlest bit.

After a few moments, Samantha found herself pedaling smoothly down the driveway. She turned a large circle and pedaled back to the front steps. "I can ride it just fine now!" she announced breathlessly. "Why, it's—it's easy!"

"I thought bloomers might do the trick," said Cornelia. "They belong to my younger sister Agnes, who was delighted to lend them to you."

"Please thank your sister for me," said Samantha, adding, "I didn't know you had a sister my own age."

"I have *two* sisters your age, Agnes and Agatha. They're twins," said Cornelia. "And a third sister who is only four years old, named Alice."

"Oh, you are so lucky to have so many sisters," sighed Samantha. "I would love to meet them someday."

"Well, Sam, I'm sure you will, because soon they'll be almost like sis—" her uncle started to say, but Cornelia shushed him.

"Shh! Not now. Later," Cornelia whispered to Uncle Gard.

"What's happening later?" Samantha asked curiously.

"Your speech at the assembly!" Uncle Gard said quickly. "So now, you must go and practice your speech. We're staying for the evening, so there will be plenty of time for cycling after the assembly."

❧

The opera house was the largest and most elegant building in Mount Bedford. It had stone pillars and an

arched window shaped like a fan above the grand front doors. Inside the carpeted lobby, students and their families, friends, and neighbors murmured greetings to one another as they filed into the large auditorium. When everyone was seated, an expectant hush fell over the room. The mayor walked onstage and welcomed the audience, and then he invited the speakers to join him on the stage. Amid polite applause, Samantha walked down the aisle and up the steps at the side of the stage, her heart beating fast. Would the audience like her speech? Would Miss Crampton be pleased or disappointed with her? And what, she wondered, would Grandmary think?

The student speakers sat in seats on the stage, facing the audience. Several students from Mount Bedford Public School spoke first, but Samantha was so nervous that she barely heard their speeches. She stared down at her own speech, which now had words crossed out and added. She tried to remember Miss Crampton's advice on elocution: *Speak slowly, clearly, and loudly. Use expression. Look at your audience.* Samantha felt relieved that Edith would go before her, since Eddleton came before Parkington in the alphabet.

Now it was Edith's turn to speak. Her speech about Kitty Hawk and the flying machines drew an enthusiastic round of applause. Then it was Samantha's turn.

With a shaky breath, Samantha stood up and walked to the front of the stage. Her heart was pounding, but she began to read her speech in a loud, clear voice. "Here in America, big cities like New York are famous for their factories," she began, describing the important and useful things that factories made, "like automobiles and bicycles. Although some people still prefer horses." Just as before,

"Some of the people who work in the factories are children,"
said Samantha. "Children as young as I am."

the audience smiled and chuckled at that line. In the front row, Miss Crampton beamed proudly.

But Samantha wasn't finished. "Some of the people who work in the factories are children," she continued. "Children as young as I am. They work long, hard hours for not much pay, and their jobs are dangerous. The factories can injure them or make them sick." Miss Crampton was no longer beaming—in fact, she suddenly looked rather pale—but Samantha plunged on. "I believe that Americans care about children and want them to be safe and healthy. Americans also want children to go to school. So if our factories would stop hiring children to work in them, then that would *truly* be proof of progress in America."

The room was silent as Samantha sat down. Beside her, Edith was red in the face. Samantha looked out at the audience. Behind her wire-rimmed glasses, Miss Crampton looked shocked, and Mrs. Eddleton's lips were tightly pursed. But in the second row, Grandmary, Uncle Gard, and Cornelia were nodding their heads.

SPEAKING AWARD

This is to Certify

That *Samantha Parkington* has completed an Outstanding Performance in Recitation and will Represent Miss Crampton's Academy for Girls in the Young People's Speaking Contest

Witness our Signatures

Given on this 8th day of October, 1904

Miss W. Crampton

Grandmary looked straight at Samantha, her eyes warm and glowing with pride as she began to clap. Uncle Gard stood up and clapped loudly. Then the whole room filled with applause.

An Act of Kindness

After the speaking contest, it was time for a bicycle ride. Samantha put on her bloomers, hopped on her bicycle, and headed off to the park, with Cornelia riding ahead of her and Uncle Gard behind. Pedaling smoothly along the paths, Samantha felt joy bubbling up in her chest. Cornelia was right—cycling was fast and free! Ahead of her, Cornelia looked back with a grin and then rode straight through a puddle, sending  a rooster tail of water spraying up on either side. Shrieking with delight, Samantha followed her through the puddle.

"It's raining, it's pouring!" Uncle Gard sputtered, as the arching spray hit his bicycle.

"Bet you can't catch me!" Samantha shouted, pedaling even faster.

"We'll see about that!" Uncle Gard called back.

Cornelia slowed to pedal beside Samantha as they rounded a turn. "Quick—take that side path, and I'll stay on this one," Cornelia whispered.

Fizzing with excitement, Samantha turned her bicycle down the narrow side path, which was nearly hidden behind dense shrubbery, while Cornelia continued pedaling along the main pathway. Ahead, Samantha saw the lake sparkling in the late afternoon sunlight. The little path was bumpy, and she had to fight to keep her balance, but it was worth it when she heard Uncle Gard asking Cornelia in a puzzled voice, "Where the dickens did Sam go?"

"Oh, she's way ahead of you," Cornelia replied serenely. "I'm afraid you'll never catch up with her."

Samantha kept pedaling. Up ahead, a wooden bridge arched over a narrow part of the lake, connecting the two banks. Samantha pedaled harder, and her momentum carried her up the bridge's slope. At the top, she stopped her bicycle. She could see Uncle Gard and Cornelia down below on the main path, which looped around a little bay and connected to the far end of the bridge. "Hello down there!" she called, waving.

Uncle Gard shaded his eyes and peered up at her. "Sam?" he called. "How on earth did you get all the way up there?"

"Follow me, and you'll see!" Cornelia said gaily, pedaling ahead and taking the loop around the little bay. Finally they all met, breathless and laughing, at the far end of the bridge.

"I may as well admit it, you two have me completely outpaced!" said Uncle Gard.

"And outsmarted!" said Samantha, sharing a conspiratorial grin with Cornelia.

Uncle Gard nodded and scratched his head in pretend exasperation. "Clearly these bloomers have turned you two into a pair of blooming geniuses on wheels. I'll never be able to keep up!" he exclaimed, as Samantha and Cornelia shook with gales of laughter.

As they rode along a shady lane back to Grandmary's house, Samantha realized happily that she had been wrong about Cornelia. Cornelia wasn't taking Uncle Gard away from her or ruining her fun with him. In fact, Samantha decided, it was quite the opposite: things were even *more* fun when Cornelia was around. *Why, I think I like Cornelia as much as my uncle does,* thought Samantha, as they rode up Grandmary's driveway and stopped at the carriage house.

Hawkins met them. "How did you do, miss?" he asked, taking Samantha's bicycle.

"I didn't fall even once," she reported.

"I knew you'd get the hang of it," said Hawkins. "And now, there's a young visitor waiting for you at the back door."

It must be Nellie, thought Samantha. She hurried to meet her, eager to tell Nellie all about her speech.

❧

"... And everyone clapped, even after I told the truth about children working in factories," Samantha said to Nellie. "Maybe it was a truth they didn't expect to hear, but they listened. And all because of you!"

Nellie didn't seem as pleased as Samantha had thought she would be. Her eyes were downcast, and she looked sad. Samantha noticed that she was no longer wearing her gray servant's dress. "Nellie, what's wrong? Has something happened?" Samantha asked.

"I've come to say good-bye. I have to leave Mount Bedford," Nellie said in a shaky voice. "I'm taking the evening train back to New York City."

"What?" Samantha exclaimed. "You are? But why?"

Nellie swallowed. "My mother has influenza, and my father needs help taking care of my little sisters." A tear rolled down her cheek.

"Oh, Nellie, I'm so very sorry," Samantha said softly. "Will you come back here when your mother is better? Or will you have to stay in the city and—and work there again?" Samantha didn't think she could bear the thought of Nellie going back to work at the thread factory.

Nellie shrugged. "I don't know," she said. Then she added tearfully, "Oh, Samantha, you're the best friend I've ever had. I'm going to miss you so much."

Samantha felt like crying, too. Nellie was truly a dear friend, even if they had to keep their friendship a secret. She hugged Nellie tightly, wishing there was something she could do to help her and her family. Suddenly, she thought of something.

"Come into the kitchen, Nellie," she said, opening the back door. Nellie hesitated. "Please come in—just for a moment." Samantha led Nellie to a chair. "Sit here, and I'll be right back." While Nellie waited, Samantha went to the pantry and whispered to Mrs. Hawkins. Then she darted up the back stairs all the way to the tower room and took Lydia from the window seat.

Returning to the kitchen, Samantha saw that Mrs. Hawkins had set a big basket of food by Nellie's feet. Now Nellie would have good food to bring home to her family. Maybe it would help her mother get well more quickly.

Samantha kissed Lydia's cheek and put the doll in Nellie's arms. "Here—take Lydia with you."

Nellie's eyes widened. "Oh no, miss—I couldn't," she said.

But Samantha insisted. "Lydia will keep you company on the journey, and when you get home, you can share her with your little sisters." Quickly, Samantha added in Lydia's pretend voice, "I want to go to the city and play with Bridget and Jenny. Maybe we can teach them to read!"

Samantha put the doll in Nellie's arms. "Here—take Lydia with you."

Nellie smiled through her tears. "Thank you," she whispered, hugging Lydia to her chest.

۞

After saying good-bye to Nellie, Samantha went up to her bedroom to rest before dinner. She felt tired, and sad for Nellie. As she lay on her bed thinking about Nellie, there was a knock on the door.

"Come in," said Samantha.

The door opened, and Cornelia stepped into her room. "I've just come to ask if you would like to keep the bloomers," she said. Then she took a closer look at Samantha. "Dear girl, are you feeling unwell?" she asked. "Is something troubling you?"

Samantha nodded. She sat up and told Cornelia all about Nellie—their secret friendship, Mount Better School, and how Nellie had taught her the truth about factories. "You see, I added that whole part to my speech *after* I was selected as a winner at school," Samantha explained.

"And you were quite right to do so," said Cornelia. "You made a brave decision, knowing that your teacher might disapprove and be disappointed in you."

Then Samantha told Cornelia about Nellie's return to the city and how she'd given Nellie her favorite doll. "Nellie loves Lydia as much as I do," said Samantha. "I know she'll take good care of her."

"How kind and thoughtful of you," said Cornelia. "I'm sure Lydia will bring comfort to Nellie and her young sisters. Now, shall I tell you about *my* sisters?" Cornelia asked.

"Oh yes, please," Samantha said eagerly. "Tell me *all* about them." She scooted to one side of the bed to make room for Cornelia, who sat down beside her.

"Well," Cornelia began, "Agnes and Agatha are identical twins. It can be hard to tell them apart! They have bright red hair and freckles, and they're both full of fun and mischief. Poor little Alice tries to keep up with her big sisters, but of course that's impossible when you're only four years old!" Cornelia smiled. "Alice means well, but she has a way of getting herself into quite a pickle at times. It must be hard to be so much younger than the rest of us."

"But still, how lovely it must be to live in a house full of sisters!" said Samantha. "Alice doesn't know how lucky she is. But someday I'm sure she will realize it."

Cornelia nodded. "Yes, we all have lots of fun together. You know, I hope that one day I will have a houseful of daughters who will have as much fun together as Agatha, Agnes, Alice, and I have."

Samantha smiled at the thought of it. "Cornelia, do you think I might visit your house someday and meet your sisters?" she asked shyly.

"Why not? I think that's a delightful idea," said
Cornelia. "Now, let's get dressed for dinner. We wouldn't
want to be late—and after all that cycling, I'm quite
famished."

❧

At dinner, Uncle Gard posed ridiculous riddles while
Elsa cleared away the dishes after each course. "Now, Sam,
what's black and white and red all over?" he asked.

"A newspaper, of course,"
said Samantha. "I already
know that one."

"Ah, but you don't! It's
a zebra with a sunburn,"
said Uncle Gard.

Cornelia rolled her eyes. Samantha laughed at her
uncle's silly riddles and jokes, but she couldn't help notic-
ing the way Cornelia kept glancing at him, as if there was
something she was waiting for him to say. Once she even
thought she saw Cornelia nudge him with her elbow. Uncle
Gard put down his fork, as if he was about to speak, but just
then Grandmary turned to Samantha and said, "My dear, I
haven't seen you with your doll Lydia lately. You two used
to be inseparable. Have you grown tired of her already?"

"No," said Samantha, "you see, I—" She broke off.
Grandmary had made it clear that she and Nellie could

never be friends, but would it really be truthful to say that she had given Lydia to Nellie in order to *help* her? Samantha swallowed. Although she did want to help Nellie and her family, that wasn't the real reason she had given Nellie her favorite doll. Samantha's heart ached as Nellie's words echoed in her mind: *You're the best friend I've ever had, and I'm going to miss you so much.* That was exactly how she felt about Nellie, and *that* was why she had given Nellie her most cherished possession. But she couldn't say that to Grandmary, so she closed her mouth and said nothing.

"Have you lost your doll, then?" Grandmary asked, as Samantha reached for a piece of bread and carefully buttered it all the way to the edges. "What a pity. She was quite an expensive doll," said Grandmary. "My dear, you must take better care of your things and learn to value them properly."

Cornelia cleared her throat delicately. "Mrs. Edwards, Samantha has given her doll to young Nellie O'Malley, whose mother is stricken with influenza. Samantha knows that Lydia will help comfort Nellie during her mother's illness."

Grandmary raised her eyebrows,

and Samantha wondered for a moment if she was angry. But when Grandmary looked at Samantha, her eyes were soft. "It is an act of kindness to give to those less fortunate than ourselves," said Grandmary. "I commend you, Samantha, for your compassion and generosity."

"Thank you, Grandmary," said Samantha, feeling greatly relieved. Perhaps her grandmother didn't know the real truth about her friendship with Nellie, but she approved of her actions, and that was what mattered.

"Well, well, well," said Uncle Gard. "Speaking of kindness and generosity, I have an announcement to make." He reached for Cornelia's hand, and Samantha noticed that Cornelia was blushing. "I must be the luckiest man in the world," Uncle Gard went on, "because Cornelia has kindly and generously agreed to be my wife. We are getting married this fall!"

Samantha felt as if her heart might burst with joy. She jumped up from her chair and ran around the table to hug her uncle. Then she turned to hug Cornelia. "Oh, I'm so glad!" she exclaimed.

"Me too," said Cornelia, hugging her back. "And we want you to be one of our bridesmaids. Will you do us that honor?"

Samantha caught her breath. A bridesmaid at their wedding! She could hardly imagine anything more wonderful. She turned to her grandmother. "May I, Grandmary?" she asked.

Grandmary was fanning herself. Her cheeks were pink and her blue eyes sparkled. Samantha thought she had never seen her grandmother looking so happy. "Of course you may," said Grandmary, folding Samantha into a hug.

Agnes, Agatha, and Alice

eady or not, here I come!" a voice called.

Samantha held her breath and tried not to move. She didn't want to give away her hiding place behind the curtain. Suddenly the curtain was thrust aside, and a freckle-faced girl grinned at her. "Oh, Agnes! You found me too soon," said Samantha, laughing.

"I'm not Agnes," whispered the girl. "I'm Agatha. May I hide with you?"

"Sure," whispered Samantha. "Squinch in."

Agatha sat so close that her curls tickled Samantha's face and made her giggle. Soon both girls were giggling so much, they didn't even hear Agnes enter the room. The curtain was thrust aside again.

"That was easy!" exclaimed Agnes. "You two made more noise than the monkeys at the zoo."

It was November, a month after the speech contest. Samantha and Grandmary were staying at the Pitt family's elegant townhouse in New York City for the week of the wedding. They had been there for three days so far, and Samantha thought it was the most fun she'd ever had.

Agnes kicked off her shoes and started jumping from bed to bed. "Come on!" she said. "Let's jump like monkeys."

"But Agnes," said Samantha, "you haven't found Alice yet."

"Oops! I forgot Alice," cried Agnes. "She always hides in the sewing room. Let's go."

The three girls rushed down the hall. In the sewing room, they could see Alice sitting on the floor under a blanket, with her feet sticking out. The older girls stifled their giggles and pretended to look for Alice for a few minutes, but when Alice began to giggle, Agnes lifted the blanket. "Why, here you are, Alice!" she said, sounding very surprised. "I found you last of all."

Alice beamed. "That means I won! Let's play again."

"No, come jump on the beds with us," said Agatha. "We'll pretend we're monkeys."

"That won't take much pretending," said a deep voice. The girls turned to see Uncle Gard and Cornelia in the doorway.

"Are you having fun with these rowdies, Sam?" Uncle Gard asked.

"Oh, yes!" said Samantha. "The most fun *ever*."

Cornelia gave Samantha a smile. "We are all delighted to have you here," she said. "Now I need you and the twins to come with me. I've something to show you."

"Our bridesmaid dresses?" asked Agnes. Cornelia smiled and nodded.

"Hurray!" shouted the twins.

"I want one, too," wailed Alice. Samantha felt sorry for her.

But Uncle Gard scooped her up, saying, "You come with me, Alice. We'll practice dancing. You are going to dance with me on my wedding day, aren't you?" Alice's face lit up, and she bounced with excitement in Uncle Gard's arms. Samantha couldn't help feeling proud of her uncle, who always seemed to know how to cheer Alice up when she was feeling left out.

The three girls followed
Cornelia downstairs to her room.
When they saw the lovely, lacy
lavender dresses lying on the
bed, they shrieked with delight—
just as Mrs. Pitt came into the
room with Grandmary.

"Great Caesar's ghost, girls!" Mrs. Pitt scolded. "Have a
care for my poor nerves!" She lowered herself into a chair
and held a handkerchief to her forehead.

"Yes, ma'am," said the girls. They couldn't wait to try
on their new dresses and were already halfway out of their
clothes.

Mrs. Pitt sighed and said to Grandmary, "I think
Agnes, Agatha, and Samantha are too young to be bridesmaids, but Cornelia insisted upon it. I do hope they'll
behave properly during the wedding."

Samantha was glad her face was hidden as she pulled
her bridesmaid dress over her head, so that no one could
see her flush. How could Mrs. Pitt say such a thing?
Samantha would *never* embarrass Cornelia—and especially
not on her wedding day.

"I'm sure they'll behave like proper young ladies,"
replied Grandmary calmly.

"Young, indeed!" Mrs. Pitt said. "They are most

exceptionally young."

"And they will be most exceptional bridesmaids," said Cornelia.

Samantha poked her head out of her dress and flashed Cornelia a grateful smile.

When all the buttons were buttoned and sashes tied, Mrs. Pitt looked at the girls with a critical eye. "You look quite presentable," she said. "Take off the dresses now. Don't wrinkle them." And with that she swept out the door.

Grandmary paused long enough to say, "You young ladies look very charming." And then she left, too.

"Cornelia," said Agatha after the girls had changed back into their regular clothes. "Please, may we see your bridal gown?"

Cornelia opened the double doors of her wardrobe, and there it was—a creamy white dream of a dress decorated with tiny pearls from its high collar to its flowing train. "And here's the best part of all," said Cornelia. From behind the gown she carefully pulled a long white cascade of lace as light and fine as mist. "My veil."

"Ooh," gasped the three girls.

Samantha sighed. "Oh, it's beautiful."

Cornelia touched the veil gently. "Isn't it lovely?" she said. "I'll wear it only once, to mark the happiest day of my life."

*It **will** be the happiest day of her life,* thought Samantha.
I'll make sure it is.

"Cornelia," said Agnes, "when I get married, may I
wear this veil?"

"Yes, of course," said Cornelia. "And you, too, Agatha.
And you, too, Samantha."

Samantha said softly, "Thank you. But I . . . I already
have a veil."

Everyone looked at Samantha with curiosity. "It was
my mother's," she explained. "Grandmary said it belongs
to me now. I've seen it only once or twice. It's in a box
in the attic in Mount Bedford."

"How wonderful," said Cornelia. "Your mother has

given you something precious to remember her by. I'm sure
it's beautiful."

"Yes," said Samantha. "It's like your veil. It's long and
white and puffy as a cloud."

Cornelia laughed. "My veil is as *big* as a cloud," she
said. "In fact, I'd better find another place to keep it. I don't
want it to be crushed." She smiled at the girls. "Well, my
exceptional young bridesmaids, run along now. I don't
want you to use up all your good behavior before the wedding. Go find Alice and get into some mischief."

But the girls weren't interested in mischief. Instead,
they decided to dress up as brides. Agatha found some old
lace curtains in the sewing room. Each girl tied one around
her waist to make a long, flowing skirt and draped another
over her head to make a veil.

Suddenly Alice appeared. "I want a bride dress and
veil, too!" she demanded. "Where's mine?"

"There are no more curtains," said Agatha. "You can be
the groom, Alice."

Alice frowned. "That's no fun!" she cried.

Samantha had to admit that Alice was right. "I'll make
you a wedding dress," she told Alice. "Wait right here."
Samantha ran down the hall to her bedroom, took a pillow
off the bed, and shook it out of its case. Then she went back
to the sewing room and pinned the lace-edged pillowcase

around Alice's waist. Alice looked happier already.

"She needs a veil," said Agnes.

Samantha looked around the room, but nothing there was lacy enough to be a veil. So she pulled off her lace petticoat and tied it to Alice's head with a ribbon as Alice, Agnes, and Agatha looked on with delight.

In their lacy costumes, the four girls practiced walking gracefully down the aisle and waltzing around the room. Samantha and the twins discovered that they could twirl and swirl and then sit down very quickly to make their skirts and veils billow out around them.

"I want to do that, too!" said Alice, disappointed because her pillowcase and petticoat didn't swirl and billow the way the older girls' curtains did.

"The next time we play dress-up, we'll make you an even better wedding dress and veil," Samantha assured her. That satisfied Alice, and the four brides played happily together all afternoon.

Alice's Wedding Dress

he day of the wedding was wintry gray and cold, but inside the Pitts' house, flowers bloomed on every table. Delicious smells floated out of the kitchen, the doorbell rang constantly, and excited voices filled the air. The four girls spent the morning upstairs smearing lemon paste on their faces to make their freckles fade. They tied their hair up in rags to make it curly. Samantha didn't actually have any freckles, and Agnes, Agatha, and Alice already had curly hair, but no one wanted to miss out on any of the fun.

About noon, the four girls wandered downstairs. When Mrs. Pitt saw their lemon-pasted faces, she cried, "Great Caesar's ghost, girls! Don't be in the way. The maid will come to help you dress at four. Until then, you older girls keep an eye on Alice." She fluttered her hands at them and said, "Shoo!"

"Yes, ma'am," said the girls. They scooted back upstairs.

Agatha asked restlessly, "What are we supposed to do all afternoon?"

"Let's play hide-and-seek," said Samantha.

"No!" said Alice. "I want to play bride."

"We'll do that next," Samantha promised. "Quick! Go hide now, Alice."

After a few minutes Samantha found Agnes and Agatha hiding under the beds. The three girls agreed that the lemon paste was making their faces itch, so they scrubbed it off. They pulled the rags out of their hair, too. They were just going to the sewing room to find Alice when Cornelia called to them.

"Come down, girls," she said. "Your bridesmaid bouquets are here!"

The girls flew down the stairs. Grandmary, Mrs. Pitt, and Cornelia were waiting for them. Cornelia held three huge bouquets of lilacs in her arms. "Here you are, ladies," she said. "Beautiful flowers for my beautiful bridesmaids."

The girls buried their faces in the bouquets to smell their lovely perfume.

Cornelia smiled and said, "Now take good care—" Suddenly the smile left her face and she gasped, "Alice!"

Everyone turned. Alice was coming downstairs draped in white from head to foot. Samantha stared, and then she gasped, too. Alice was wearing Cornelia's wedding veil!

Alice was wearing Cornelia's wedding veil!

She had torn it in two and used one part for a skirt and the other part for a veil. The lace hung in tatters. Cornelia's veil was ruined—completely, utterly, totally ruined.

"Great Caesar's ghost!" exclaimed Mrs. Pitt.

"No," said Alice cheerfully. "I'm not a ghost. I'm a bride! Now I have a swirly skirt, too!"

For a moment, no one moved or said a word. Then Grandmary groaned. Mrs. Pitt collapsed into a chair. Agnes and Agatha wailed, "Oh, Alice!" Alice burst into tears. She could tell she had done something terribly wrong. Cornelia was very pale.

"You older girls go to your room," said Grandmary quietly.

The three girls trudged upstairs and flopped onto their beds. *If only we'd known Cornelia put her veil in the sewing room this morning!* thought Samantha. *We could have warned Alice not to touch it. But now . . .* "We've got to do something," she said in a determined voice.

"What can we do?" asked Agatha. "The veil is ruined. We can't fix it."

"And it's almost one o'clock. The wedding's in four hours," Agnes pointed out. "There's not enough time to get a new veil."

"Not a new veil," said Samantha slowly. "An old veil. I have a plan."

Samantha found Uncle Gard in the study. He listened to her carefully. When she finished, he looked at his pocket watch and shook his head. "It's awfully risky, Sam," he said. "I'm not sure there's enough time, especially in this icy weather. We don't want Cornelia to come down the aisle with no veil only to find she has no groom, either."

Samantha was impatient. "Please, Uncle Gard. We've got to try."

Uncle Gard stood up. "You're right, Sam. We do have to try. Let's go!"

A Most Exceptional Bridesmaid

amantha held her coat over her head as she rushed out of the house and climbed into Uncle Gard's automobile. Sleet slashed at the windshield. Soon Samantha was being bounced and bumped as the automobile lurched along the icy, rutted roads. Uncle Gard was driving fast. Even so, it seemed to Samantha that the trip was taking ages.

When they finally pulled up to Grandmary's house in Mount Bedford, Samantha hardly waited for the motorcar to stop before she jumped out and ran up the slippery steps. She hammered on the door with both fists and called out, "Hawkins! Elsa! It's me! Hurry! Someone open the door!"

Elsa opened the door and exclaimed, "Miss Samantha! Sakes alive! Whatever's going on?"

Samantha did not stop to explain. She ran past Elsa and pounded up the stairs to the attic. She pushed hatboxes, shoe boxes,

and dusty boxes of books out of her way until she found it—the box holding her mother's veil.

Samantha lifted the lid and looked at the delicate veil. It smelled faintly of rose petals, a smell that always made her think of her mother, Lydia. The soft smell of roses was reassuring. It was as if her mother were giving her blessing to the idea of letting Cornelia wear her veil.

Samantha closed the box and carried it down the stairs and out to the automobile. She and Uncle Gard did not talk much on the trip back to the city. Samantha knew it must be getting late because the sky was darkening. *Please let us get back in time,* she thought. *Please!*

❧

At half past four, Samantha and Uncle Gard walked into the Pitts' town house—and into an uproar. "Where on earth have you two been?" cried Mrs. Pitt. She pushed her way toward them through a swarm of maids and musicians, waiters and florists. Samantha left Uncle Gard to explain. She hurried up the stairs to Cornelia's room and tapped on the door.

"Why, Samantha!" said Cornelia when she opened the door. She was already wearing her wedding gown. "Everyone's been worried. Where have you been?"

"I have something for you, Cornelia," said Samantha. She set the box on the floor, knelt beside it, and opened the lid. "It's my mother's veil."

Cornelia sank to her knees next to Samantha. Slowly, she lifted the veil out of the box. "Oh," she sighed. "It's so beautiful! I am honored to wear it." Cornelia had tears in her eyes, but she laughed as she said, "Oh, thank you, Samantha, thank you!"

❧

Candles glowed in every window. The music began. Mrs. Pitt, Alice, and Grandmary sat smiling in the first row of chairs. Exactly on cue, first Agnes, then Agatha, and then Samantha walked down the flower-lined aisle to the graceful arch of greenery in front of the Pitts' hearth.

Uncle Gard stood by the hearth next to the minister. His hair was still damp, and his tie looked as if he had tied it in a hurry. But he looked happy. His smile broadened as the three girls walked toward him. He winked at Samantha.

Everyone murmured in awe as Cornelia came slowly down the aisle on her father's arm. Samantha thought she seemed almost to float in her dress. Through the fine lace of the veil, Cornelia smiled at Uncle Gard. Then she, too, winked at Samantha. Samantha felt her heart fill with love as she and Agnes and Agatha stood shoulder to shoulder—three most exceptionally happy bridesmaids.

Samantha felt her heart fill with love.

In 1904, the United States was entering a brand-new century, and the country was bursting with change. Cities were getting bigger, and buildings were getting taller. Automobiles were taking the place of horses. Lightbulbs were being used instead of gas lamps. Inventions like electric irons, vacuum cleaners, stoves, phonographs, and telephones were changing the way people worked and lived.

New construction towered above the surrounding buildings.

Well-to-do families like Samantha's lived in large, comfortable houses. They visited with their guests in fancy parlors where children were often not allowed. When children did join the adults in the parlor, proper behavior was expected. A girl like Samantha would curtsy and say, "How do you do?" She would speak

An elegant parlor was no place for children to play.

only when an adult spoke to her first. Meals were served in elegant dining rooms, the table set with delicate china plates, heavy crystal glasses, and crisply ironed cloth napkins.

The elegance and comforts of proper life were possible because there were many servants to do the work. A cook like Mrs. Hawkins spent nearly all day making meals for a family from scratch, since there were very few convenience foods like cake mix or canned soup. A maid like Elsa scrubbed the floors and cleaned the rugs. A servant like Hawkins tended the garden and took care of the horses and carriage that people used instead of a car.

The lives of servants were not very elegant or comfortable. They worked long days for little money. Servants were expected to keep their "proper" place—separate from the family they worked for. They ate separately and often lived in small rooms in the attic or above the carriage house.

Without electric dryers or irons, laundry was hard work!

Servants were not supposed to visit with the parents or play with the children.

Even though a servant's life was hard, there were plenty of people willing to do these jobs. Many of the people living in American cities were poor. They would do any kind of work just to help their families survive. If they weren't servants, they often worked in factories for long hours and little pay. Samantha was shocked when Nellie told her about the work she had done in a factory. Children as young as three years old worked twelve-hour days, six days a week. They gave the money they earned to their mothers and fathers to help pay the rent or buy food.

Working in these factories was dangerous and unhealthy. Inside a cotton mill, the air was hot, humid,

This mother made 75 cents a day working until midnight. Instead of going to school, her daughters worked with her.

and dusty. The humidity kept the thin threads from breaking, but it was unhealthy for the children who worked there. Many became ill with lung disease. The roar of the machines was so loud that anyone inside had to scream to be heard.

These children worked barefoot in a textile factory.

Even though there were laws that said children should not work, many families desperately needed money and sent their children to work anyway. Some children tried to work during the day and go to school at night, but often they were so tired that they fell asleep at their desks.

Young ladies like Samantha did not work. Washing dishes, sweeping floors, and making beds were not considered proper tasks for them to do. When they weren't in school, girls spent their time learning fancy needlework,

practicing piano, reading, painting, and playing with toys such as dolls and tea sets.

At the turn of the century, girls and women were starting to play sports and games that were previously only played by men and boys.

A three-year-old standing next to an enormous machine in a factory

Imagine playing tennis in a fancy dress!

Ladies enjoyed lawn tennis and field hockey, but they still wore long skirts and lace-up boots. Even when they went swimming, girls and women wore a bathing dress and silk stockings.

Bicycling, which was a popular pastime, prompted some ladies to change their style of clothing. They started wearing *bloomers,* or full pants gathered at the knee, to make riding easier. Like Grandmary, some people didn't think bloomers were appropriate for women. Others felt the same way Cornelia did: "a lady behaves like a lady no matter what she's wearing."

It was easier to ride a bike wearing bloomers (above) *than skirts* (below).

Lost and Found

❧ CHAPTER 1 ☙

New York City! Just the name was magic! As a special treat for her tenth birthday, Samantha Parkington and her grandmother, whom she called Grandmary, had taken the train from Mount Bedford to New York City. Now they were riding along the busy city streets from Grand Central Station to Uncle Gard and Aunt Cornelia's new house. Samantha leaned forward to peek out the window of the horse-drawn cab. She held on to her hat and twisted her head around, trying to see to the tops of the buildings. Everything in New York was so big! There were so many people hurrying along the sidewalks. In New York it always seemed as if something exciting was about to happen.

"I can't wait to see Agnes and Agatha," Samantha said to Grandmary. The twins were Cornelia's younger sisters. Now that Uncle Gard and Cornelia were married, Agnes and Agatha were Samantha's newest friends and favorite relatives. "They're so much fun."

"They are happy, lively girls," agreed Grandmary. "Though they can get carried away with their ideas."

Samantha understood what Grandmary meant about Agnes and Agatha. Sometimes their ideas were as tangled as their bouncy red curls. "They're always thinking up new ways to do things," Samantha went on.

"Yes," said Grandmary. "But I'm afraid they don't always think very carefully. Besides, they don't realize that many times the old ways are still the best ways."

Suddenly, the cab jerked to a stop. Grandmary and Samantha looked out the window. They were stopped at the edge of a big park. The sidewalk was so crowded that people spilled out into the street. Samantha saw some women hanging large banners across the entrance to the park. One banner said "WOMEN,  FIGHT FOR YOUR RIGHT TO VOTE." Another banner said "NOW IS THE TIME FOR CHANGE."

"We'll have to go another way, ma'am," the cab driver called down to Grandmary. "These ladies seem to be blocking traffic all around Madison Square Park."

"Very well," Grandmary answered, sitting back. She didn't seem to want to look at what was going on.

But Samantha pressed her nose against the window of

the cab and stared. She was fascinated. "What's happening here?" she asked Grandmary.

"Well, it appears that a group of women is having a meeting in that park," Grandmary replied.

"Who are they?" Samantha asked.

"They're suffragists," Grandmary answered. "They think women should be able to vote, so they gather and make a ruckus about changing the laws." She sat up very straight. "It's all just newfangled notions."

The cab turned down a quieter street and Samantha sat back. She was still very curious about the meeting in the park, but she could tell by the look on Grandmary's face that she should not ask any more questions about it.

They rode in silence until the cab stopped in front of Uncle Gard and Aunt Cornelia's tall, narrow brownstone house. Samantha had just hopped out onto the sidewalk when she heard voices shouting, "Samantha! Samantha!" She looked up. Agnes and Agatha were leaning out of a  window high above her, waving wildly. Agnes held up Cornelia's lively little dog, Jip, and waved his paw. Jip barked and wriggled with joy.

"Hello!" Samantha called. She skipped and waved, already swept away by the twins' high spirits.

"We'll be right down!" Agatha yelled. Then she and Agnes and Jip disappeared from the window.

Cornelia smiled as she came down the front steps to Samantha and Grandmary. "Welcome!" she said. Just then the twins and Jip came flying out the door and down the steps. "Hurray! You're here!" they said as they hugged Samantha. Aunt Cornelia laughed. "Come in, come in," she said. "As you can see, we're all very glad you're here."

The twins led Samantha into the dark, cool house. Uncle Gard was waiting just inside the doorway. He blinked at Samantha and said, "There you are, Sam! I've been looking for you all week long. I can't seem to find anything in this new house."

"Do you think you could help us find some lunch?" asked Aunt Cornelia.

"Certainly," said Uncle Gard, kissing the tip of her nose. "When it comes to finding food, I never have any trouble."

"Come on, Samantha!" said Agnes and Agatha. They pulled her into the dining room and made her sit between them. Then, both at once, they began showering her with questions. "How was your train ride? Do you want to go to the park after lunch? Do you want—"

"Girls!" Aunt Cornelia scolded gently as the maid began to pass the food. "You'll put Samantha in a spin

with all your questions! There will be plenty of time
for chatter later. I haven't even had a chance to ask
Grandmary where she plans to shop today."

"I'll shop at O'Neill's, of course," replied Grandmary.
"I never go any farther."

"There's a fine new shop on Fifth Avenue that's closer
than O'Neill's," said Uncle Gard. "What was the name of
that store, Cornelia?"

Grandmary patted his arm and smiled. "Don't trouble
yourself to remember, Gardner," she said. "I shall go to
O'Neill's. I've shopped there for more than thirty years.
I'm too old to change my ways now."

"O'Neill's is near Madison Square Park," said Aunt
Cornelia slowly. "That area may be quite crowded today.
There's a meeting in the park."

"I know," said Grandmary. "We passed it on our way
from the station. Those suffragists were
already blocking traffic." She shook her
head. "In my opinion, ladies should not
gather in public places. *Especially* not to
carry on about this voting nonsense."

"Nonsense?" Aunt Cornelia asked.
Her voice rose ever so slightly.

"Voting is not a lady's concern," said Grandmary. It
never has been. I see no reason to change things now.

Those suffragists are making spectacles of themselves."

Samantha saw Agnes and Agatha look at each other with raised eyebrows and then quickly look down into their soup bowls.

Aunt Cornelia opened her mouth to say something and then shut it again.

Samantha was bursting with curiosity. "But why—?" she began to ask.

"Well, well, well," interrupted Uncle Gard. "Well, well. The strangest thing happened to me as I was walking home from work the other day. A man came up to me and said, 'Do you know any girls who just turned ten years old?' And I said, 'Why, yes, in fact I do know one.' And he said, 'Would you give her this large box? There's something inside she might like.' So I brought the box home. It's out in the hall. Perhaps you'll open it, Sam, and show us what's inside."

Samantha forgot all about her questions. She and the twins ran from the table and opened the dining room door. Jip was waiting right outside. He barked and jumped as the twins helped Samantha tear off the wrapping paper and open the box. Inside was a pram—the prettiest doll carriage Samantha had ever seen. It was deep red with shiny brass wheels. "Jiminy!" Samantha whispered. "It's beautiful." She ran to give Uncle Gard a

big hug. "Thank you, Uncle
Gard. Thank you very much!"
She knew perfectly well the
doll carriage was from Uncle
Gard and no one else.

Uncle Gard winked. "Happy Sam Day, Bertha," he
said. "Oops! I mean, happy birthday, Samantha!"

"Let's take it to Gramercy Park right now," suggested
Agnes, who was as excited as Samantha.

"That *would* be fun," Samantha said. "May we go?"

"Certainly," said Uncle Gard.

"Can Jip come, too?" asked Agatha. "You know how
he loves the park."

"No, I don't think that is a good idea," said Aunt
Cornelia. "He might run away from you."

"Oh, no, nothing like that will happen," said Agatha
quickly. "Anyway, the park has a fence all around it."

"Please, please, please?" begged Agnes.

Aunt Cornelia thought for a moment.

"We'll only be across the street in the park," wheedled
Agatha.

"And you won't go any farther than that?" asked Aunt
Cornelia.

"No!" the twins promised together.

"Will you keep Jip on his leash?"

"Yes!" shouted the girls.

"Promise?"

"Absolutely!" they cried.

"Well, all right," Cornelia finally agreed. "But—"

"Hurray!" the twins interrupted. Jip began yipping in excitement.

"Please be calm for just a minute," Aunt Cornelia said seriously. "I'm going to a meeting, but I'll be back at three thirty. When I get back, we'll walk to the ice cream parlor to meet Grandmary. Don't forget."

"And don't forget to behave like young ladies," added Grandmary.

"And don't forget the rule about keeping Jip on the leash," repeated Aunt Cornelia.

"And don't forget to have a good time," said Uncle Gard, shaking his finger at them.

"We won't!" said the girls. And Jip barked to show that he agreed.